Three Ways to Trap a Leprechaun

Library of Congress Control Number: 2019932660
ISBN: 978-0-06-284128-5

Typography by Brenda E. Angelilli
19 20 21 22 23 SCP 10 9 8 7 6 5 4 3 2 1
❖
First Edition

Three Ways to Trap a LEPRECHAUN

By Tara Lazar

Pictures by Vivienne To

HARPER

An Imprint of HarperCollinsPublishers

My little brother, Sam, doesn't think leprechauns are real—can you believe that?

Well, I believe in leprechauns. They're magical, mischievous, miniature marvels! It's almost St. Patrick's Day, so it's time to show Sam the inescapable truth. . . .

I'll build an inescapable leprechaun trap!
Time to plan, plot, and plow ahead with my design.

Do I have the proper tools and supplies? Let's find out . . .

TA-DA!
Welcome to my leprechaun trap laboratory.
Pretty snazzy, huh?

In this trap the stick holds the basket, the string is tied
to the stick, and something shiny is attached to the string.
No leprechaun can resist this trap.
Let's give it a test run.

Now it's zero hour, countdown
to Claire the hero hour.
Let's lure a leprechaun . . .

OH, ZIP!

He tripped the trap but gave us the slip!
Hey, what's this note?

Try and try, but
I'll be gone.
You can't catch me—
I'm a leprechaun
—Finn

Ha, Finn sounds like the Gingerbread Man
right before the fox got him!
Well, I'm sly like a fox, too! I can outfox Finn.

BACK TO THE LAB!

That last trap's kaput. It was far too simple, Sam!
I need a wild roller coaster of a trap.
I'll twist this twine . . . and loop and wind Finn in circles.

Don't take a nap. I'll nab him now!

Finn got loose and vamoosed! But how?

Try and try, but
let me be clear.
Your machine
is missing a gear.

Hmm . . . I've designed, I've built, I've tested.
He's vanished every time. What am I not seeing?
Wait, **THAT'S IT**—a trap Finn doesn't see!

I'll disguise my trap!
I need mirrors like a fun house . . .
a spool of invisible wire . . .

But then we blinked—and we were hoodwinked!
In a twinkle, Finn the Leprechaun was gone.

I'd like to say my work here is done. But now
I've got a lab assistant. And that's a good thing . . .

. . . because we're gonna need a **Bigger Trap!**

SO YOU WANT TO CATCH a

Everybody knows that the night before St. Patrick's Day is your best chance at trapping one of these magical, mischievous, miniature marvels! Here are Claire's tricks for catching your own leprechaun. . . .

HERE ARE SOME SUGGESTIONS FOR SUPPLIES TO HELP!

- 🍀 Cardboard box (like a shoebox or cereal box)
- 🍀 Anything shiny, like foil or shiny coins
- 🍀 Construction paper
- 🍀 Pipe cleaners
- 🍀 Markers, crayons, or paint
- 🍀 Popsicle sticks
- 🍀 Glitter
- 🍀 Tape or glue
- 🍀 Tinfoil
- 🍀 Paper towel roll
- 🍀 Confetti
- 🍀 Rubber bands
- 🍀 Ribbons
- 🍀 Paper clips
- 🍀 Mirrors
- 🍀 Any other leprechaun bait you can think of!

Leprechaun? 🍀

1. DO YOUR RESEARCH. Leprechauns are tricky, so you have to be **EVEN TRICKIER** to catch one! One great way to lure a leprechaun is to think of the stuff leprechauns love best—like gold, clovers, rainbows, and all things green or sparkly! Brainstorm a list of all the things a leprechaun might love.

2. SKETCH IT. Now that you have a list of ideas to tempt your leprechaun into a trap, how are you going to snag him? Claire came up with some cool ideas. . . . What are yours? Grab some paper and a pencil and start designing!

3. GATHER YOUR SUPPLIES. You'll need all the leprechaun lures you just brainstormed, and all the pieces to build the trap, too. (See the list for some suggestions!)

4. BUILD, BUILD, BUILD! Time to put all your good ideas into motion.

5. TIME TO WAIT. This is the hardest part of all! But the leprechaun won't sneak up until you're long gone. Sounds like it's time for bed.

🍀 **Happy Trapping!**